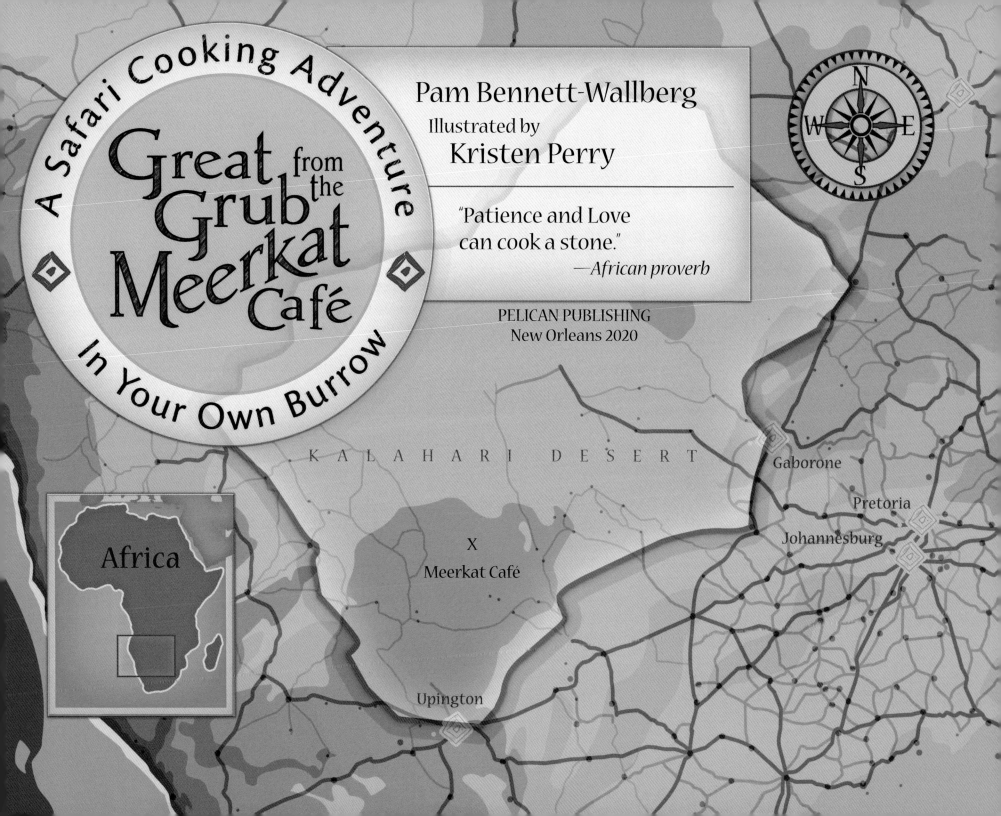

A Safari Cooking Adventure

Great Grub from the Meerkat Café

In Your Own Burrow

Pam Bennett-Wallberg

Illustrated by
Kristen Perry

"Patience and Love
can cook a stone."
—*African proverb*

PELICAN PUBLISHING
New Orleans 2020

Africa

KALAHARI DESERT

Gaborone

Pretoria

Johannesburg

X
Meerkat Café

Upington

Although all the animals in this book can safely eat the insects used in the recipes, we do *not* recommend that you do!

ISBN 9781455625116
Ebook ISBN 9781455625123

Printed in Malaysia

Published by Pelican Publishing
New Orleans, LA
www.pelicanpub.com

Contents

The Kalahari Desert —
A hungry and
thirsty land...

Introduction

Blueprints
Meerkat Café

Under Construction
Meerkat Café
~COMING SOON!~

Food For Thought

A meerkat can move 80 pounds of dirt in a day.

Meerkats have 4 very long, non-retractable claws on their front feet. The claws are shorter on the back feet.

Each of their eyes has a nictitating membrane (a third eyelid) that shields them from dirt while digging.

A meerkat's ears also close tightly to keep out sand and dirt.

Meerkats know the exact location of all the burrows and bolt holes in their tunnel system so they can quickly dash below ground to safety.

"United friends eat from the same plate."
— *African proverb*

After a busy day of working, a meerkat family enjoys sitting together to watch the sun set and to groom each other.

Young meerkats would rather play, but all members of the family must share the work.

Meerkat pups are important to the future of the "mob." Litter size ranges from 2–7 pups and they are usually born between April and October which are the warmer, wetter months in southern Africa's Kalahari Desert.

The gestation period for meerkats is 77 days.

"Being true friends, even water drunk together is sweet."
—*African proverb*

Welcome guests to the Café's Grand Openi...

6

Sunrise Specials

Food For Thought

Meerkats dig their burrows in hard, compacted soil rather than loose sand which would easily collapse. All members of the family, except very tiny pups, help with the chore of excavating the burrows, bolt holes, and tunnels.

Meerkats sometimes allow ground squirrels to live with them in their burrows because the squirrels "pay rent" by helping the meerkats dig the burrows and watch for predators.

Mature male and female meerkats "scent mark" the family's burrow with anal scent glands to tell other meerkat mobs to stay away. It's like a chemical *no trespassing* sign.

Meerkats are diurnal—daytime animals. But meerkats are not early risers. They prefer to sun bathe before they begin foraging.

Meerkats have dark skin on their sparsely-furred tummies that they use as "solar panels" to warm up.

In Africa a meerkat is called a "sun angel." In Germany a meerkat is called an "Erdmannchen" which means "little earth man."

"While sun is shining, bask in it."   —*African proverb*

Tok Tokkie Beetle Breakfast Casserole

- ¾ cup (90.5 grams) chopped Tok Tokkie beetles. If you are counting calories, use only the female beetles. (Or chopped pecans will do.)

- 2 teaspoons (9.562 grams) butter

- 4 cups (436.00 grams) peeled, sliced Golden Delicious apples

- 6 Tablespoons (71.86 grams) granulated sugar

- Cooking spray

- 12 slices of cinnamon-swirl bread, cut in half diagonally

- 1 ½ cups (354.9 milliliters) milk

- ½ teaspoon (1.257 grams) ground cinnamon

- 5 large eggs

- 1 Tablespoon (11.98 grams) granulated sugar (to sprinkle over casserole before baking)

- Maple syrup to serve with casserole

"One beetle talks to another."

—*African proverb*

Serves 8

Melt butter in large skillet.

Add apples and 1 Tablespoon (11.98 grams) sugar to the skillet. Sauté and stir for 8 minutes or until the apples are tender. Remove from heat and set aside.

Coat a 9 x 14 inch (33 x 23 centimeter) glass dish with cooking spray. Arrange half of the bread in the dish.

Top bread with apple mixture. Top apple mixture with ½ cup (60.33 grams) Tok Tokkie beetles (or pecans).

Arrange remaining bread over Tok Tokkie beetles (or pecans). Set aside.

Combine 5 Tablespoons (59.89 grams) sugar, milk, cinnamon, and eggs in a bowl. Stir well with a whisk.

Pour milk mixture over bread. Press bread firmly down to cover with liquid.

Cover and refrigerate overnight.

The next morning: Preheat oven to 350 degrees F (175 degrees C). Uncover dish. Sprinkle ¼ cup (30.17 grams) of Tok Tokkie beetles (or pecans) over the bread mixture. Sprinkle 1 Tablespoon (11.9 grams) sugar over the casserole.

Bake for 45–48 minutes or until a knife inserted into the center comes out clean.

Serve with maple syrup.

Food For Thought

Male Tok Tokkie beetles thump their bums on the ground to make a tapping sound (tokking) in order to attract a mate. If he's lucky, the female will tap back.

There are many species of Tok Tokkie beetles and each has its own distinctive "tap" pattern.

To get a drink of water, some species climb a sand dune, do a headstand facing west so fog condenses on their backs and trickles into their mouths.

A few Tok Tokkie species dig trenches in the western face of a sand dune and wait for the condensation of water to accumulate.

Some species of the beetle have extra-long legs to keep them off the hot sand.

Their thick, chitin shells keep the moisture in and the heat out.

They make burrows in the sand.

Dung Beetle Pancakes

- 8 dung beetles (well-washed because they are *dung* beetles). (Or, 8 fully cooked Brown 'N Serve sausages.)

- 1 ½ cups flour (187.4 grams)

- 3 Tablespoons granulated sugar (35.93 grams)

- 1 teaspoon salt (5.02 grams)

- 1 ¾ teaspoon baking powder (6.555 grams)

- 1 egg

- 3 Tablespoons melted butter for the batter (43.03 grams)

- 1 ¼ cups milk (295.7 milliliters)

- Butter to spread on the pancakes

- Maple syrup

Makes 10–12 pancakes
Mix the flour, sugar, salt, and baking powder.

Beat egg slightly then add butter and milk.

Slowly blend in the dry ingredients.

Heat electric griddle to 375 degrees F (190 degrees C).

Cut the dung beetles (or the Brown 'N Serve sausages) into thin slices. Then, place in skillet and cook until brown.

When cooking the pancakes, press the sliced dung beetles (or the sliced sausages) into the batter. Turn the pancakes over and cook the other side.

Serve with butter and maple syrup.

Food For Thought

Dung beetles eat poop. But, they are fussy about the kind of poop they eat. They prefer poop from herbivores which is largely undigested plant material. The poop from carnivores has very little nutritional value for dung beetles.

Dung beetles roll poop into a ball and push it to their burrow by using their back legs. Dung beetles roll their balls of poop in straight lines by using the Milky Way as a compass.

Surprisingly, some dung beetle species give excellent parental care to their young. Both parents equally care for their young by digging the nest together. Some species even mate for life.

Dung beetles frequently live in hot, sunny places so they will often climb on top of the dung ball to let their feet cool off.

"Every Dung Beetle is a gazelle in the eyes of its mother."

—*African proverb*

Fruit Fly Smoothie

- 1 cup (225.00 grams) of mashed fruit flies. (Or, if you're out of flies, you can use one banana.)

- 1 cup (240 milliliters) plain yogurt

- ¼ cup (60 milliliters) strawberry jam

- 4 ice cubes

Serves 1
Place the fruit flies (or banana peeled and cut into chunks), yogurt and jam into a blender.

Cover. Blend until mixed. Add ice cubes and blend until smooth.

"Flies come to feasts unasked."

—*African proverb*

Food For Thought

Fruit flies fend off "body-snatching" wasps by drinking alcohol. Wasps like to invade the bodies of fruit flies and lay their eggs in them. But, the fermented juice of rotting fruit (6% alcohol) that the fruit flies drink will kill the parasitic wasps when they try to lay eggs inside the flies. Cheers!

Fruit flies have red eyes (maybe from all the alcohol) and they can beat their wings 220 times per second.

Fruit flies are used in laboratories to study genetics and diseases.

Female fruit flies are larger than the males.

A fruit fly has a hairy body and very sticky feet.

A fruit fly can lay up to 100 eggs a day. In her lifetime, she can lay 2,000 eggs. That's a lot of babies!

Fruit flies can live up to 30 days in the wild, but its life span can be extended three times if it lives in a laboratory.

Fruit flies like to "hang out" around ripe fruit, wine, garbage and trash cans.

The eyes of a fruit fly have 760 individual lenses.

Two thirds of a fruit fly's brain is used for visual processing.

Oatmeal with Lice

- 3 Tablespoons (30.17 grams) of lice—keep them away from your hair! (Or, you can use toasted sesame seeds.)

- ½ cup (75.71 grams) raisins

- 1 ¼ teaspoons (6.284 grams) salt

- 2 cups (160.9 grams) old-fashioned rolled oats (not instant)

- ⅓ cup (56.78 grams) whole, toasted almonds

- 1 cup (236.6 milliliters) chunky applesauce (heated)

- Honey to serve with oatmeal

- Milk to serve with oatmeal

"A louse in the food is better than no food at all." —*African proverb*

Serves 6

In a medium saucepan, bring 4 cups (946.4 milliliters) of water and the salt to a boil.

Stir in the oats and raisins. Boil gently, stirring frequently for 7 minutes. Remove from heat.

Stir in the almonds. Cover pan and let stand for 3 minutes.

To serve: Layer oatmeal and applesauce in 6 bowls. Drizzle with honey and sprinkle with lice (sesame seeds will do) and serve with milk.

Food For Thought

A female louse can lay 120 eggs per month. That's lousy!

Adult lice are about the size of sesame seeds. The nit (egg) is the size of a pencil lead.

Lice can't jump, hop, or fly. But, they can crawl about 450 feet per day which is longer than a football field.

Lice aren't nice! But, even people with good hygiene can get lice.

Research confirms that having lice is often a sign that the person is very friendly and outgoing.

Lice eggs will camouflage themselves to match hair color. Clever!

Lice feed by injecting saliva into a person's scalp and sucking the blood out.

The lice's saliva allows blood vessels to expand and stops blood from clotting.

Lice feed every few hours. Yummy!

Lice can live happily in eyelashes and eyebrows, too!

Head lice have been around a very long time. They have been found on Egyptian mummies.

Lice are true survivors and can live underwater for several hours.

Lice eggs attach to hair with a glue-like substance.

Lice are real "party animals" and are most active at night.

Lice do not discriminate. They love people of all ages, races, and economic backgrounds.

Cockroach French Toast

- 10 slices of freshly baked cockroach bread. (Or, you can use raisin bread but it won't be as moist.)

- 2 eggs

- 1 cup (240 milliliters) orange juice

- 1 ½ cups (241.3 grams) of crushed vanilla wafers

- Butter

- Powdered sugar

- Maple syrup

Serves 5
Beat the eggs and orange juice together with a fork.

Dip the cockroach bread (or raisin bread) slices into the egg mixture and then into the vanilla wafer crumbs.

Grease the griddle with butter and heat to 375 degrees F (190 degrees C).

Cook the bread on one side until golden brown.

Flip and cook the other side. Add more butter to the pan as needed.

Place on a platter and sprinkle with powdered sugar.

Serve with butter and maple syrup.

Food For Thought

Talk about "losing your head!" Cockroaches can survive without their heads for a week. They do have brains, but their brains don't control all of their vital functions. Most of the organs that control a cockroach's vital functions are found in the thorax which is in the middle of its body.

Cockroaches have been around longer than dinosaurs so cavemen had problems with them, too.

There are about 4,600 species of cockroaches and they are found on every continent except Antarctica. One species of cockroach can even live in the desert. When there is an absence of water, the cockroach absorbs water from the air by using its mouth structures.

Cockroaches can hold their breath for 40 minutes. (No scuba tank needed!) They take in air though small holes in their bodies, but they are able to close these holes when immersed in water.

Cockroaches can live for weeks without food.

Cockroaches can run 3 miles per hour. They can also race up walls by running faster than they do on flat surfaces. The spines on their legs help them "stick" to slippery surfaces.

"If you dishonor people in this life, you will come back as a cockroach."

—*African proverb*

High Noon Highlights
Food For Thought

Meerkats have dark markings around their eyes that act like built-in sunglasses.

Meerkats loose heat easily which helps keep them cool in the heat of the desert.

Their burrows are dug 6–8 feet deep in stable ground to keep the meerkats comfortable. Not too hot, not too cold, just right.

Meerkats will lie with their stomachs flat on the ground to cool off. That position is called "hearth rugging" because the animals look like rugs in front of a fireplace hearth.

The burrow and tunnel systems vary in size. The largest systems have up to 90 entry/exit holes and the smallest have less than 10. Meerkats always try to stay close to a burrow or bolt hole to avoid predators. If the weather is very cold or very hot, the meerkats will spend a portion of the day in their cozy underground home.

"The afternoon knows what the morning never suspected."
—*African proverb*

Creamy Parastizopus Beetle Chowder

- 6 Parastizopus beetles, chopped. (Parastizopus beetles are expensive, so you can use 6 slices of *lean* bacon cut into very small pieces.)

- 1 small onion, thinly sliced

- 2 cups (402.2 grams) of raw potatoes, peeled and diced

- 1 can 14.75 ounces (418 grams) cream-style corn

- 1 ½ cups (354.9 milliliters) milk

- 2 Tablespoons (28.69 grams) butter

- 1 ¼ teaspoons (6.284 grams) salt

- ½ teaspoon (1.996 grams) granulated sugar

- ⅛ teaspoon (0.29 grams) pepper

Makes 6 servings

In a large sauce pan, cook the Parastizopus beetles (or the bacon) until cooked but *not* crisp.

Add the onion to the beetles (or the bacon) and cook until the onion is golden.

Add the potatoes and ¾ cup (177.4 milliliters) water. Bring to a boil. Boil gently and stir frequently for about 10 minutes until the potatoes are tender but not mushy.

Add the corn, milk, butter, salt, sugar, and pepper. Simmer, covered about 10 minutes or until hot.

"In the desert even a beetle is meat."
—*African proverb*

Food For Thought

After heavy rains the Parastizopus beetles mate and lay their eggs in a burrow in the sand. After just two days the eggs hatch and the mother beetle brings the larvae foliage from the bloubos (blue bush) plants into the burrow for the young to eat. The larvae also feed on a substance secreted from the mother's body, without which they cannot survive.

Parastizopus beetles are monogamous. The males and females have different jobs. The males do most of the burrow digging, maintenance of the burrow, and cleaning of the pupae. The females do most of the food gathering. The female will also guard the burrow when not foraging for food.

The burrow is guarded from intruders by a secretion from the beetle's abdomen.

The eggs, larvae, and pupae need almost 100% humidity to develop and hatch.

The depth of the burrow is one of the most important factors in successful rearing of the young.

Large males can dig deeper burrows and, thus, the eggs stay moister.

Tampan Tick and Egg Salad Sandwiches

- ⅓ cup (73.34 grams) of squashed ticks. (Mayonnaise will work, but it won't be as tasty.)

- 2 Tablespoons (30.0 grams) of finely chopped sweet pickles

- 2 Tablespoons (16.27 grams) of finely chopped onion

- 1 ½ Tablespoons (22.185 milliliters) of sweet pickle juice

- ½ teaspoon (2.514 grams) salt

- ½ teaspoon (2.612 grams) of prepared mustard (not dry mustard)

- ⅛ teaspoon (0.29 grams) pepper

- 8 large, hard-boiled eggs (chilled), finely chopped

- 8 slices of bread

- Lettuce

Makes 4 sandwiches
In a large bowl combine all the ingredients (except the eggs) and mix well.

Add chopped eggs and mix until well blended.

Spread on bread and add lettuce.

Food For Thought

Africa's tampans are soft-bodied ticks that are often associated with camelthorn trees because of the tick's habit of burying themselves in the dirt under the shade of the trees. The ticks wait patiently for their victim to sit down in the shade of the tree. The ticks then emerge to feast on the blood of the animal or the person.

Some ticks can live a long time without eating. If a tick can't find a host to feed upon, it will go into a "dormant" stage.

Some tick species inject their hosts with an anesthesia so the victim won't feel the bite and the tick can feed without disturbance.

Ticks are little blood-sucking vampires.

Ticks are not insects. They are arachnids and are the close relatives of spiders and scorpions.

Ticks like to feed on their hosts for a long time. They bite into the skin of the host with their curved teeth and often stay attached for days.

"The donkey carries the load, but it is the tick that complains."
—*African proverb*

Buckspoor Spider Sandwiches

- 9 ounces (240 grams) of buckspoor spiders (remove the legs so they don't get caught in your teeth). (Or, use 9 ounces (240 grams) of canned deviled ham.)

- 4 ounces (113 grams) cream cheese (Not whipped. Use "solid block" cream cheese.)

- 1 cup (110.00 grams) coarsely grated carrots

- 1 cup (226.80 grams) finely chopped yellow bell pepper

- 1 cup (160 grams) finely chopped onions

- 1 cup (180 grams) sliced black olives

- 6 to 8 taco-sized, flour tortillas

Makes 6–8 sandwiches

Mix the buckspoor spiders (or deviled ham) and the cream cheese in a bowl.

Spread the mixture evenly on 6 to 8 tortillas.

Sprinkle ½ of each tortilla with the carrots, bell pepper, onions, and olives.

Fold each tortilla in half. Then, fold the tortilla again to make a triangular-shaped sandwich.

Food For Thought

The clever female buckspoor spider makes a nest in sandy soil that looks like the tracks of an antelope.

The silk-lined tunnel leads from the center of the web into the ground.

She spins silk and places sand on it so the web is almost invisible. The trapdoor on the web has several depressions which look like the footprint of an antelope.

The female waits in her lair. A single strand of silk detects vibrations and the spider rushes out to overpower the prey that is crossing her web.

The male and female buckspoor spiders look very different. The female is bigger and is a different color. The female is sedentary while the male is fond of racing around on the hot sand. Both males and females are most active when it is very hot.

"When spider webs unite they can tie up a lion."
—*African proverb*

Sloppy Stink Bugs on Buns

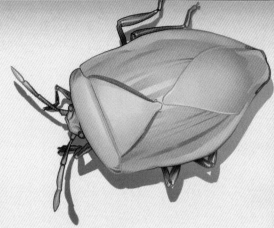

- 1 pound (450 grams) of ground stink bugs. Wash these little stinkers at least three times. (Although it's not nearly as tasty, 1 pound (450 grams) of ground beef will do.)

- ½ cup (56.68 grams) chopped green pepper

- 1 small onion, chopped

- 8 ounce (230 grams) can tomato sauce

- ½ cup (118.3 milliliters) catsup

- 1 Tablespoon (13.75 grams) of firmly packed brown sugar

- 1 teaspoon (2.415 grams) dry mustard

- ¼ teaspoon (1.257 grams) salt

- ⅛ teaspoon (0.29 grams) pepper

- 1 Tablespoon (14.79 milliliters) Worcestershire sauce

- 1 Tablespoon (14.79 milliliters) vinegar

- Hamburger buns

- Softened butter to spread on buns

Makes 4–5 servings

In a large skillet brown the stink bugs (or ground beef), green pepper, and onion. Drain some of the excess fat.

Stir in remaining ingredients (except the hamburger buns). Simmer, uncovered for 20 minutes. Stir occasionally.

Serve over toasted, buttered hamburger buns.

Food For Thought

Stink bugs got their name because they release a smelly odor when they are protecting themselves. Some people describe the odor as smelling like stinky feet.

Some species of stink bugs are really awesome mothers. Mama stink bug will protect her eggs and defend them from predators.

A stink bug's worst nightmare is a small, parasitic wasp that lays her eggs inside stink bug eggs. A single wasp can lay her eggs in several hundred stink bug eggs which then never hatch.

After baby stink bugs hatch from their eggs they gather around the broken egg shells and begin sucking on the shells to get several necessary nutrients.

"Do not tell the donkey that is carrying you he stinks."
—*African proverb*

Sun Spider Bundles

- 14 large sun spiders (with legs removed). (Or, two 4 ounce cans (226 grams) of drained, albacore tuna will work in a pinch.)

- 1 cup (101 grams) of very finely chopped celery

- ½ cup (60.33 grams) of grated cheddar cheese

- 1 small onion, finely chopped

- ½ cup (118.3 milliliters) of mayonnaise

- Salt and pepper to taste

- 8 hamburger buns

- Softened butter to spread on buns

Makes 8 sandwiches

In a large bowl mix all of the ingredients except the hamburger buns.

Butter the hamburger buns.

Fill the buns with the sun spider mixture (or the tuna mixture).

Wrap each sun spider bundle in aluminum foil.

Place the bundles on a baking sheet.

Bake at 350 degrees F (180 degrees C) for 15 minutes.

Food For Thought

The sun spider is a nocturnal solifugae. The name solifugae means "one who flees from the sun." It runs quickly across the sand, but "freezes" immediately when it detects danger. Often it frightens people by seemingly chasing them, but all the sun spider is trying to do is stay in a person's shadow and, thus, keep out of the intense sunlight. It is non-venomous, but its strong jaws can give a painful bite.

A female sun spider is a very good mother. After she lays her eggs in a burrow she will stay with the eggs until they hatch.

The female sun spider can grow to 3–6 inches in length. The male is extremely small in comparison to the female. In fact, the fully grown males are often mistaken for young sun spiders.

Sun spiders are also called wind scorpions and camel spiders. They prefer to live in hot, dry habitats.

If they feel threatened, the sun spider can run about 10 miles per hour.

Sometimes the females use human hair to line their burrows.

Sun spiders are primarily nocturnal and they can use stored fat on their bodies to survive when food is scarce.

If they are threatened they make a hissing sound.

"If you close your eyes to facts, you will learn little." —*African proverb*

Sunset Staples

Food For Thought

When they are cold, meerkats fluff up their fur to trap warm air next to their bodies. They will also fluff up their fur to make themselves look larger and more intimidating to predators. They can even fluff the fur on their tails.

Meerkats have the ultimate "Napoleon Complex" —they are small but mighty. Adults stand 12 inches tall and weigh 2 pounds.

Meerkats use different calls to identify various predators and to communicate with each other. They can growl, murmur, spit call, cluck, peep, bark, chirp, and trill. Females are more vocal than males.

Meerkats do not see well at night, so it is important for them to be safe and snug in their burrows at night.

Meerkats are matriarchal—Girls Rule!

"Do not rush the night —the sun will always rise for its own sake."

—*African proverb*

Burritos with Frantic Tortoise Beetles

- 2 (16 ounce) (454 grams *each*) cans of smashed frantic tortoise beetles. (These beetles are hard to find so don't get frantic. You can use 2 cans of "traditional flavor" refried beans.)

- 1 (17.5 ounce) (496 grams) package of burrito-sized flour tortillas

- 1 large tomato, diced

- 12 lettuce leaves, sliced thinly

- 1 avocado, sliced

- 8 green onions, sliced

- 1 (4.5 ounce) (127 grams) can of sliced black olives, drained

- 2 teaspoons (2.4 grams) dried onion flakes

- ½ teaspoon (1.676 grams) dried, minced garlic

- 1 teaspoon (5.028 grams) salt

- ¼ teaspoon (.55 grams) ground cumin

- 1 teaspoon (2.415 grams) chili powder

- ¼ teaspoon (.45 grams) oregano

- 4 teaspoons water (19.715 milliliters)

- 1 (16 ounce) (453 grams) package of shredded cheddar cheese

- 1 (8 ounce) (225 grams) container of sour cream

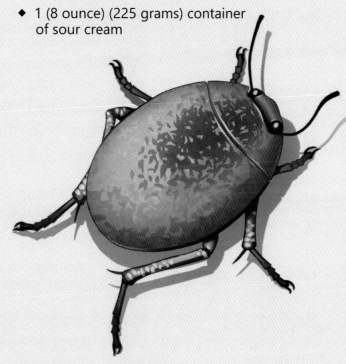

Food For Thought

The frantic tortoise beetle has a waxy covering that is used to help water retention, thermoregulation, and predator avoidance. These beetles are always running around "frantically" on hot surfaces.

They are also called "Koffiepits."

Makes 6–8 servings

On a very large serving platter arrange the tomatoes, lettuce, avocado, green onion, and olives.

Empty the cans of frantic tortoise beetles (or refried beans) into a large microwave-safe bowl. In a small bowl mix the dried onion flakes, dried garlic, salt, cumin, chili powder, oregano and stir well.

Add the dry seasoning mix to the frantic tortoise beetles (or the refried beans) and add 4 teaspoons (19.72 milliliters) of water. Stir very, very well and cover the bowl.

Heat the frantic tortoise beetle mixture (or refried bean mixture) for 2 minutes in the microwave.

Take a tortilla and spread a thin layer of smashed frantic tortoise beetles (or refried beans) on half of the tortilla.

Spread sour cream on the other half of the tortilla.

Sprinkle on cheese and add the other ingredients from the serving platter.

Fold the tortilla in half. Then, fold the tortilla again to make a triangular-shaped burrito.

"Beetles do not live in a busy door hinge."

—*African proverb*

Millipedes and Cheese

- 1 cup (227 grams) of millipedes cut into pieces. Clip a clothes pin on your nose because millipedes give off a very foul odor when handled. (Or, you can substitute 8 ounces (227 grams) of uncooked macaroni.)

- ½ cup (60.33 grams) of dried bread crumbs

- 4 Tablespoons (57.37 grams) of melted butter

- 1 small onion, finely chopped

- 1 Tablespoon (7.807 grams) flour

- ¼ teaspoon (0.6038 grams) dry mustard

- 1 teaspoon (5.028 grams) salt

- ⅛ teaspoon (0.29 grams) pepper

- 1 ½ cups (354.9 milliliters) milk

- 2 cups (241.3 grams) of shredded cheddar cheese

- 6 slices of cheddar cheese to melt over each portion just prior to serving

Makes 6 servings

Cook macaroni as label directs. Drain well.

Heat oven to 350 degrees F (175 degrees C).

Grease 9 x 9 x 2 inch (23 x 23 x 5 centimeter) square baking dish. In a small bowl combine bread crumbs with 2 Tablespoons (28.69 grams) of melted butter.

Put remaining melted butter (2 Tablespoons or 28.69 grams) in a saucepan. Add onion and cook until tender (about 5 minutes).

Slowly add flour, mustard, salt and pepper. Stir well.

Slowly add milk. Cook, stirring constantly, until thickened to the consistency of pancake batter.

Remove pan from heat.

Add cheese. Add millipedes (or add the cooked macaroni). Mix well.

Spoon mixture into baking dish. Sprinkle bread crumbs over the top of millipedes (or macaroni).

Bake 20 minutes until top is golden brown.

Let stand for 8 minutes.

Before serving, melt one slice of cheddar cheese over each portion.

Food For Thought

The name millipede comes from two Latin words—mil meaning "thousand" and ped meaning "feet." But, millipedes don't have a thousand. In fact, most millipedes have less than 100 legs. The millipede species that has the most legs still has only 750.

Millipedes leave tracks of two distinctive lines with many dots that are close together.

Some millipedes practice chemical warfare. They don't bite or sting, but some species have stink glands that emit a foul smelling compound that repels predators.

Millipedes are surprisingly long-lived. They move slowly, are well-camouflaged, and can live up to 7 years.

"Two footprints do not make a path." —*African proverb*

Spaghetti with Grasshopper Heads

- 10 ounces (284 grams) of frozen grasshopper heads. Remove the antennae. (If you don't have time to remove all the antennae, you can always substitute 10 ounces (284 grams) of frozen peas.)

- ½ pound (227 grams) of thin spaghetti

- 3 Tablespoons (43.03 grams) butter

- 3 Tablespoons (23.42 grams) flour

- ½ teaspoon (2.514 grams) salt

- ¼ teaspoon (0.45 grams) of cayenne pepper

- 2 cups (473.2 milliliters) milk

- 2 cups (241.3 grams) of grated cheddar cheese

- 2 teaspoons (9.858 milliliters) of Worcestershire sauce

- ⅛ teaspoon (0.99 grams) of Tabasco sauce

- 6 slices of bacon cooked crisp in the microwave. Use paper towels to absorb the grease.

- Grated parmesan cheese to top

Makes 4 servings

In a medium sauce pan melt the butter. Blend in flour, salt and pepper.

Cook the mixture on low heat for one minute.

Gradually add the milk to the mixture.

On medium heat, stir constantly and cook the mixture until it boils and thickens.

Slowly stir in the grated cheddar cheese.

Add the Worcestershire sauce.

Add the Tabasco sauce.

Stir and heat over medium heat until the mixture is smooth and the cheese is melted. Cover the pan to keep the sauce warm.

Cook the bacon and set aside.

Thaw the frozen grasshopper heads (or the frozen peas) in room temperature water. Drain.

In a large pot cook the spaghetti as directed on box.

Add the thawed grasshopper heads (or the thawed peas) to the sauce. Re-warm the sauce.

Drain water from the cooked spaghetti.

Put spaghetti on plates and top with sauce, grated parmesan cheese, and crumbled bacon.

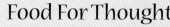

Food For Thought

Male grasshoppers make a singing sound by rubbing a hind leg against one of their forewings. The leg causes the wing to vibrate and make a sound like a bow on violin strings.

Grasshoppers hear with their abdomens.

Grasshoppers have wings used for flying. Grasshoppers, in large groups, are called locust. During migrations to find more food, grasshoppers can remain in the air without landing for three days.

"Don't ride an elephant to catch a grasshopper." —*African proverb*

Chili with Blister Beetles

- 15 ounce (425 grams) can of blister beetles (do *not* drain the juice). (Or, if you prefer a milder chili, you can use 15 ounces (425 grams) of un-drained kidney beans.)

- 1 pound (450 grams) of ground beef

- 1 celery stalk, chopped

- 1 medium onion, chopped

- 3 teaspoons (6.018 grams) chili powder

- 1 teaspoon (5.028 grams) salt

- Dash of pepper

- One 14.5 ounce (411 grams) can of stewed tomatoes

- 8 ounce (225 grams) can of tomato sauce

- Grated cheddar cheese to top each portion

Makes 6 servings

In a large skillet brown the ground beef, onion, and celery.

Stir in remaining ingredients except the blister beetles (or kidney beans).

Stir well.

Add blister beetles (or kidney beans).

Simmer covered for 30–45 minutes until flavors are blended. For a thicker chili cook uncovered for the last 10 minutes.

Top each portion with grated cheese.

Food For Thought

Adult blister beetles secrete liquids that contain the poison cantharidin from their leg joints.

Cantharidin will blister human skin. Medicinally, cantharidin is used to remove warts.

Some blister beetle larvae will attach themselves to bees which carry the beetles back to the bee hive. Then, the sneaky beetle eats the members of the hive.

Worldwide there are approximately 2,500 blister beetle species.

When hay is harvested in the field blister beetles might be ground up in the harvesting equipment. The cantharidin poison then taints the hay and if horses or other livestock eat the hay they can become sick or die.

"In his own nest a beetle is a chief." —*African proverb*

Sticky Cricket Legs

- 12 huge cricket legs. (Or, 12 regular chicken drumsticks can be used because cricket legs can be very tough.)

- ½ cup (162.5 milliliter) apricot jam

- ¼ cup (72 grams) teriyaki sauce

- 1 Tablespoon (13.75 grams) dark brown sugar (packed down)

- ¼ teaspoon (1.257 grams) salt

- 1 teaspoon (5 milliliters) cider vinegar

- 1 teaspoon (3.13 grams) cornstarch

Makes 6 servings
Heat oven to
350 degrees F
(175 degrees C).

Remove the skin from the cricket legs (or, the drumsticks).

In a large bowl mix the jam, teriyaki sauce, brown sugar, salt and vinegar. Slowly add the cornstarch. Mix well.

Add the cricket legs (or, drumsticks) and coat well.

Place the cricket legs (or, drumsticks) in a shallow pan. Bake for 15 minutes. Remove the cricket legs from oven and (with a pastry brush) coat them with more sauce. Return to oven. Bake 60 minutes longer. Brush with sauce and turn the legs every 10 minutes.

Place cricket legs in a serving dish and spoon sauce over all.

"The cricket is never blinded by the sand when digging its burrow."
—*African proverb*

Food For Thought

Dune crickets have unusually large feet which enhance their digging ability and also act as "snow shoes" when they walk over sand dunes.

Crickets hear with their knees.

Only male crickets produce a "song." Males have "toothed" areas on their wings which produce a chirping sound when the cricket rubs its wings together.

Males chirp to attract a female. However, males can also produce a different chirp that is used as a sign of aggression toward other males.

The number of chirps a male cricket produces depends on the outside temperature. The warmer the temperature the more chirps a male produces.

To calculate the outside Fahrenheit temperature: Add 37 to the number of chirps a cricket produces in 15 seconds. I wonder if this is how the weather man does it.

Crickets have wings but they can't fly. Grounded!

Crickets have excellent eyesight.

Crickets are nocturnal. They do not have long life spans.

In some cultures crickets are considered to be a sign of good luck.

Customer Favorites

- ½ cup (162.5 milliliters) of smashed red velvet ants. (Or, you can use ½ cup (162.5 milliliters) of strawberry jam, but the color will be rather pale in comparison to the red velvet ants.)

- 1 ¾ cups (218.6 grams) flour

- ½ cup (95.82 grams) granulated white sugar

- 1 Tablespoon (11.24 grams) baking powder

- ½ teaspoon (2.514 grams) salt

- 2 eggs lightly beaten

- ⅔ cup (157.7 milliliters) milk

- ⅓ cup (76.49 milliliters) butter, melted

- 1 teaspoon (3.155 grams) grated lemon zest

Pangolin's Favorite... Muffins *with* Red Velvet Ant Filling

Makes 12 muffins
Heat oven to 400 degrees F (204.4 degrees C). Grease the bottoms only of a muffin pan.

Mix together all the dry ingredients. Combine the beaten eggs, milk, melted butter, and lemon zest. Stir the liquid mixture into the dry mixture. Stir just until the flour is moistened. The batter will be a little lumpy. Don't over mix.

Fill muffin cups half full of batter. Drop a teaspoonful (5 milliliters) of jam in the center of the batter. Add more batter over the jam to fill the muffin cups ⅔ full.

Bake at 400 degrees F (204.4 degrees C) for 18–20 minutes until golden.

Food For Thought

A pangolin's scales are made of keratin which is the same protein that makes up human fingernails. Their scales cover the entire body from head to tail. The belly of a pangolin is only covered in a few sparse hairs. So, when threatened, a pangolin curls up into a tight ball to protect itself.

Pangolins can close their ears and nostrils to protect themselves from insects. They also have very thick eyelids to protect themselves from insect bites.

Although a red velvet ant looks cute and fuzzy, it doesn't mean that it is friendly. In fact, the ant can inflict a very painful sting. The species come in a variety of colors: White, blue, black, silver, and red.

Pangolins do not have teeth. Instead, they have long sticky tongues which catch their insect prey.

Pangolins can eat 23,000 ants per day.

"In watching for the ant, don't let the elephant pass unnoticed." —African proverb

Kori Bustard's Favorite...
Centipedes *in* Blankets

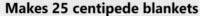

- 25 large centipedes (removing all the legs will take some time). (Or, 25 miniature hot dogs.)

- 1 ¼ cup (156.1 grams) *self-rising* flour

- ½ cup (118.3 milliliters) whole milk

- 2 Tablespoons (28.69 grams) butter, melted

- 1 large egg and 2 teaspoons (9.858 milliliters) of water slightly beaten together to be used as an egg wash

---

> "The crocodile drinks from the same river as the centipede."
>
> —*African proverb*

Makes 25 centipede blankets

Heat oven to 425 degrees F (218.3 degrees C).

Lightly grease a cookie sheet.

In a large mixing bowl combine the flour, milk, and melted butter until a ball of dough forms.

Roll the dough into a thin rectangle about ¼ inch thick (6 millimeters) on a lightly floured surface.

Cut the dough lengthwise into 1 inch (2.5 centimeters) strips.

Using a fork, prick each centipede (or the miniature hot dog) twice.

Dry the centipedes (or the miniature hot dogs) with a paper towel.

Place one centipede (or miniature hot dog) on the end of the strip of dough and roll it twice to "blanket" it. Cut the dough and press gently to seal the loose end.

Place it "sealed side down" on the cookie sheet. Repeat with all the other centipedes (or miniature hot dogs).

Brush each "blanketed" centipede (or miniature hot dog) with the egg wash.

Bake for 12 minutes or until golden brown. Serve with ketchup and mustard.

Food For Thought

Male kori bustards are the world's heaviest flying birds and have deep, booming calls.

Kori bustards prefer to stay on the ground and generally only fly to escape danger.

These enormous birds do not have a preening gland which produces an oily substance to clean some birds' feathers. So, the kori bustard takes dust baths to keep its feathers free of parasites.

Centipedes have venomous claws to subdue their prey.

Centipedes continue to molt even as adults. So, if a centipede losses a leg, it will simply regenerate the leg with each molt.

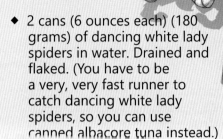

Drongo's Favorite...
Dancing White Lady Spider Casserole

"The spider knows what it will gain by being clever."
—*African proverb*

- 2 cans (6 ounces each) (180 grams) of dancing white lady spiders in water. Drained and flaked. (You have to be a very, very fast runner to catch dancing white lady spiders, so you can use canned albacore tuna instead.)
- ½ cup (29.57 grams) of crumbled, fresh bread crumbs (about 1 slice of bread)
- 1 Tablespoon (3.80 grams) of chopped, fresh parsley
- 4 Tablespoons (57.37 grams) of butter
- 2 cups (132.5 grams) of fresh, sliced mushrooms
- ¼ cup (38 grams) finely chopped green onion
- ¼ cup (25.25 grams) finely chopped celery
- ¼ cup (37.25 grams) finely chopped red pepper
- ⅓ cup (41.64 grams) flour
- 3 cups (710 milliliters) milk
- 8 ounces (230 grams) wide egg noodles. Cooked as label directs
- 1 teaspoon (5.028 grams) salt
- ⅛ teaspoon (0.29 grams) pepper

Makes 6–8 servings
Heat oven to 375 degrees F (190 degrees C). Butter a 2 quart (23 x 23 x 4 centimeter) baking dish.

Combine breadcrumbs and parsley.

In a saucepan melt butter over medium heat. Add mushrooms, green onion, celery, and red pepper. Stir and cook until tender. Turn heat off and slowly add flour. Turn heat back on. Stir and cook for one minute.

Slowly add milk and mix well. Stir and cook until it boils. Reduce heat to a simmer. Stir and cook mixture for one minute.

In a large bowl combine the sauce, dancing white lady spiders (or tuna), cooked noodles, salt and pepper. Pour mixture into buttered baking dish. Sprinkle with bread crumbs.

Bake for 25 minutes until the bread crumbs are browned.

Food For Thought

Drongos have learned to imitate the alarm calls of meerkats. The drongo will sit in the trees above the foraging meerkats until they catch something. Then, the drongo screeches the mimicked alarm call which sends the meerkats diving for cover and abandoning their food. The drongo then swoops down and steals the meerkats' hard-earned meal.

A dancing white lady spider builds a burrow out of silk in the slip face of a sand dune which it closes with a small silk trap door. If threatened by predators it jumps off, curls into a ball, and rolls down the dune at an astonishing speed. It has huge fangs and can inflict a painful bite, but its venom is mild.

Hoopoe's Favorite...
Assassin Bug Bread

- 1 cup (151.4 grams) chopped up assassin bugs. (Or, if you prefer, use 1 cup (151.4 grams) of chopped dates, but the bread will not be as crunchy.)

- ⅓ cup (76.49 grams) butter, softened

- ¾ cup (143.7 grams) granulated sugar

- Softened butter or cream cheese to spread on baked, sliced bread

- ¾ cup (177.4 milliliters) buttermilk

- 2 cups (249.8 grams) flour

- ½ cup (57.96 grams) chopped walnuts

- ½ teaspoon (2.144 grams) baking soda

- ½ teaspoon (1.873 grams) baking powder

- ½ teaspoon (2.514 grams) salt

- 2 eggs

Makes 1 loaf
Grease the bottom only of a 9 x 5 x 2 inch (23 x 13 x 8 centimeters) loaf pan.

Heat oven to 350 degrees F (175 degrees C).

In a large bowl blend the butter and sugar together.

Beat the eggs and add to butter and sugar mixture.

Blend in the buttermilk.

In a separate bowl, mix the flour, nuts, baking soda, baking powder, salt, and the assassin bugs (or, the chopped dates). Add the dry mixture to the moist ingredients.

Stir until the dry ingredients are just moistened.

Pour batter into the pan.

Bake at 350 degrees F (175 degrees C) for 49–50 minutes. Cool for 8 minutes in the pan.

Remove bread from pan and cool completely before cutting. Spread slices of baked bread with softened butter or cream cheese.

"Procrastination assassinates action."
—*African proverb*

Food For Thought

The female hoopoe is responsible for hatching the eggs and the male feeds her during the incubation period. The nest is made in the cavities of trees or rocks.

The female hoopoe secretes a foul substance that smells like rotten meat which keeps most predators away, but attracts insects which is their main diet.

Assassin bugs inject digestive juices into their prey's body and wait for the internal organs to turn to liquid and then they suck it up like a milk shake.

Assassin bugs are clever hunters. If they want to eat termites they use dead termites to attract live ones. Some assassin bugs cover their legs with tree resin to attract bees.

Aardwolf's Favorite...
Termite Casserole

- 1 pound (454 grams) of diced harvester termites. (It can take *days* to "harvest" enough harvester termites to make this recipe, so you can substitute 1 pound (454 grams) of lean ground beef.)

- 3 cups (680.39 grams) of peeled, thinly sliced white potatoes

- 10 ½ ounces (298 grams) of condensed cream of mushroom soup

- 1 cup (160.00 grams) of finely chopped onions

- 3 cloves of garlic, peeled and finely minced

- ¾ cup (177.4 milliliters) milk

- 1 cup (120.7 grams) of shredded cheddar cheese to top the casserole

- 1 teaspoon (2.1 grams) coarsely ground pepper

- 1 teaspoon (5.028 grams) salt

- 1 teaspoon (1.60 grams) dried tarragon

Food For Thought

An aardwolf is a member of the hyena family. It has a broad tongue that is coated with sticky saliva which enables the animal to lap up to 200,000 termites a night. An aardwolf prefers to hunt for termites (which are one of their main food sources) on still, dry nights which are best to hear their prey. The patter of rain drops interferes with hearing the termites.

An aardwolf has a very impressive threat display. It can bristle its mane and tail fur to increase its silhouette by more than 70%.

Harvester termites forage for grasses and other plant material by night during the hot months and by day during the cold months. The aardwolf changes from being nocturnal to diurnal to coincide with the termites' schedule.

Termite mounds are massive, long-lived structures that can be 6 feet high and 65 feet in diameter. Plants often grow next to termite mounds because of the large amount of "frass" (termite poo) that is distributed around the mounds.

"Small termites collapse a roof."
—*African proverb*

Serves 6
Preheat oven to 350 degrees F (177 degrees C).

In a large skillet over medium heat, brown the harvester termites (or 1 pound (454 grams) of lean ground beef) with the onions and garlic.

In a bowl combine the condensed mushroom soup, milk, salt, pepper, and tarragon. Mix well.

In a 2 quart (2 liter) baking dish alternately layer potatoes, soup mixture and meat several times until the potatoes, soup mixture, and meat are gone.

Bake for 1 hour and 15 minutes or until the potatoes are tender.

Remove from oven. Sprinkle shredded cheese over the casserole.

Continue baking for about 5 minutes more until cheese is melted.

Bat-Eared Fox's Favorite...
Cicada Meat Loaf

- 1 ½ pounds (680 grams) of freshly ground cicadas. (If you are out of cicadas, 1 ½ pounds (680 grams) of ground beef can be substituted, but the meatloaf will not be as yummy.)

- ⅓ cup (40.22 grams) of dry bread crumbs

- 1 teaspoon (5.028 grams) salt

- ¼ teaspoon (0.57 grams) pepper

- 1 small onion, very finely chopped

- ⅓ cup (78.85 milliliters) catsup

- 1 teaspoon (4.929 milliliters) Worcestershire sauce

- 1 egg

Makes 5–6 servings

In a large bowl combine all ingredients. Mix well.

Press mixture into a greased 8 x 4 inch (22 x 11 x 6 centimeter) loaf pan.

Bake at 350 degrees F (175 degrees C) for 1 hour.

Let stand for 5 minutes. Lift onto serving platter and cut.

Food For Thought

Bat-eared foxes have huge, 5-inch ears that are full of blood vessels which shed the heat ("ear conditioning") and for exceptional hearing —"insect radar."

Bat-eared foxes have 8 extra molars to grind up the hard body casings of insects. This brings their total number of teeth to 48.

Cicadas live on every continent except Antarctica. They live most of their lives underground but, when they emerge, they are bad flyers and often bump into things.

Male cicadas make very loud noises with their tymbals to either attract females or keep predators away.

> "A mantis stalking a cicada is unaware of the bird lurking behind it."
> —*African proverb*

Yellow-Billed Hornbill's Favorite...
Rhinoceros Beetle Breakfast Muffins

- ◆ 4 Large rhinoceros beetles thinly sliced. (Rhinoceros beetles can be very tough if they are old, so you can use 4 slices of bacon instead.)

- ◆ 20 ounces (450 grams) of frozen hash browns, *thawed*

- ◆ 4 Tablespoons (57.37 grams) of melted butter

- ◆ ½ cup (60.33 grams) shredded cheddar cheese

- ◆ 12 large eggs

- ◆ Salt and freshly ground pepper

"However much the beetle is afraid, it will not stop the bird from eating it." —*African proverb*

Makes 12 muffins
Preheat oven to 400 degrees F (205 degrees C).

Use cooking spray to grease muffin pans.

Cut the rhinoceros beetles (or the 4 strips of bacon) into small pieces. Cook until crisp. Drain on paper towels and set aside.

Combine the hash browns, melted butter, and cheddar cheese in a large bowl.

Divide the mixture into 12 muffin tins. Firmly press the mixture down and up the sides with a spoon to create "bowls."

Bake for 28–30 minutes until brown and crispy. Let cool slightly.

Crack an egg into each hash brown cup. Season with salt and pepper and top with crumbled rhinoceros beetles (or crumbled bacon).

Bake for an additional 12–15 minutes. Serve warm.

Food For Thought

The yellow-billed hornbill was made famous by the Disney movie called *The Lion King*. The bird was used as the character named Zazu.

When the female yellow-billed hornbill is ready to lay eggs she enters a hole in a tree and then closes the hole with her poo, leaving only a small slit. The male hornbill feeds her through the slit while she incubates her eggs.

Male rhinoceros beetles use their horns to fight other males. Females do not have horns.

Rhinoceros beetles are the strongest beetles on Earth. Some species can lift an object 850 times their own weight.

Warthog's Favorite...
Ground Locust Vegetable Soup

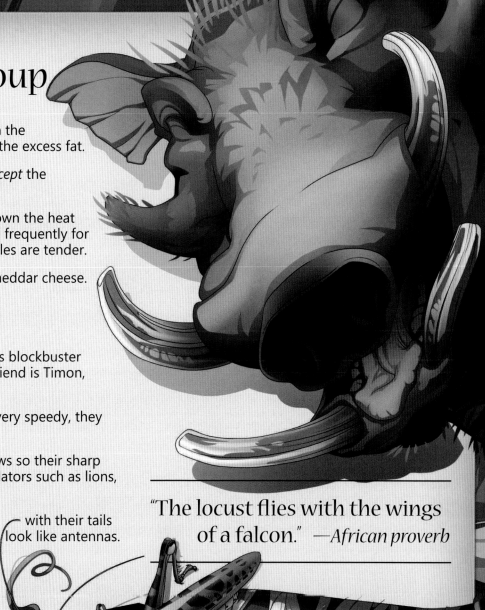

- 1 pound (450 grams) ground locusts (remove the wings or they will get stuck in your teeth). (Or, 1 pound (450 grams) of ground beef can be used if you can't collect enough locusts.)

- 2 teaspoons (10.06 grams) salt

- ½ teaspoon (0.9 grams) pepper

- 2 teaspoons (3.2 grams) tarragon

- 2 medium carrots, sliced

- 1 medium potato, cubed

- 1 medium stalk celery, sliced

- 1 medium onion, chopped

- 4 cups (946.4 milliliters) of water

- 2 Tablespoons (14.79 milliliters) Worcestershire sauce

- 14.5 ounce (411 grams) can of tomatoes, undrained and cut into small pieces

- Grated cheddar cheese to top each serving

Makes 6–8 servings

In a very large, deep pan brown the locusts (or ground beef). Drain the excess fat.

Stir in remaining ingredients *except* the cheese.

Bring to a boil and then turn down the heat and simmer, uncovered, stirring frequently for 25 minutes or until the vegetables are tender.

Top each serving with grated cheddar cheese.

Food For Thought

Pumbaa is a warthog in Disney's blockbuster movie *The Lion King*. His best friend is Timon, the meerkat.

Although warthogs don't look very speedy, they can run 35 miles per hour.

Warthogs back into their burrows so their sharp tusks can be used to deter predators such as lions, leopards, and hyenas.

Warthogs, very comically, run straight up in the air which with their tails look like antennas.

When locusts fly together, the swarm can be miles wide, blotting out the sun, and devouring ever plant in its path.

"The locust flies with the wings of a falcon." —*African proverb*

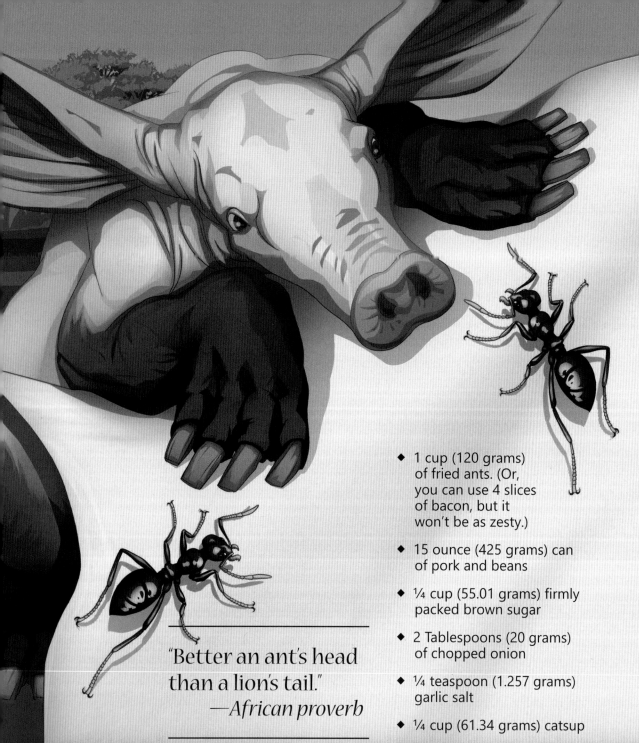

Aardvark's Favorite...
Ants *and* Beans

Serves 4

In a skillet fry the ants until crisp. (Or, cut the bacon into very small pieces and fry until crisp.)

Combine the other ingredients with the ants (or, bacon).

Place mixture in a 1 quart (946.4 milliliter) casserole.

Bake uncovered for 30 minutes at 350 degrees F (175 degrees C).

Food For Thought

The aardvark's name means "earth pig" in Afrikaans, but it is not related to pigs.

An aardvark can eat up to 50,000 ants in one night. The aardvark's tongue is 1 ½ feet long. They have ears like a rabbit, webbed feet like a duck, claws like a bear, and a tail like a kangaroo.

Most ants can carry 20 times their own body weight. And they have 2 stomachs. They don't have lungs. Oxygen enters through tiny holes all over their bodies.

Ants are the longest living of all insects. Some species live up to 30 years.

- 1 cup (120 grams) of fried ants. (Or, you can use 4 slices of bacon, but it won't be as zesty.)

- 15 ounce (425 grams) can of pork and beans

- ¼ cup (55.01 grams) firmly packed brown sugar

- 2 Tablespoons (20 grams) of chopped onion

- ¼ teaspoon (1.257 grams) garlic salt

- ¼ cup (61.34 grams) catsup

"Better an ant's head than a lion's tail."
—*African proverb*

Sociable Weaver's Favorite...
Flea Crisp with Apples

- ¾ cup (165 grams) firmly packed fleas. (Brown sugar will work if you can't find enough fleas.)

- 6 cups (654 grams) peeled, sliced cooking apples

- 1 Tablespoon (14.79 milliliters) lemon juice

- 1 Tablespoon (14.79 milliliters) water

- ½ cup (62.46 grams) flour

- ½ cup (40.22 grams) old-fashioned rolled oats (not instant)

- 1 teaspoon (2.514 grams) cinnamon

- ½ cup (114.7 grams) butter (chilled)

Makes 6 servings

Place apples in an 8 inch (20 centimeter) square pan.

Sprinkle apples with lemon juice and water.

In a small bowl, combine fleas, (or brown sugar), flour, oats, cinnamon, and chilled butter (slice the chilled butter into thin slivers) and mix until crumbly.

Sprinkle mixture over the apples.

Bake at 375 degrees F (190 degrees C) for 40–45 minutes. Cool to room temperature before serving.

"Do not strike a flea on a lion's head." —*African proverb*

Food For Thought

Sociable weavers build enormous, haystack-like nests that can reach 15 feet in height and 25 feet in length. The nests are made in tall trees or on tall structures such as telephone poles.

Sociable weaver colonies consist of 100–300 pairs of birds. Both parents and young siblings help to raise the chicks. Sociable weavers also help care for unrelated chicks in the colony.

A female flea can lay 2,000 eggs in her lifetime.

Fleas feed on blood and can live for 100 days without a meal.

A flea can jump 150 times its own height.

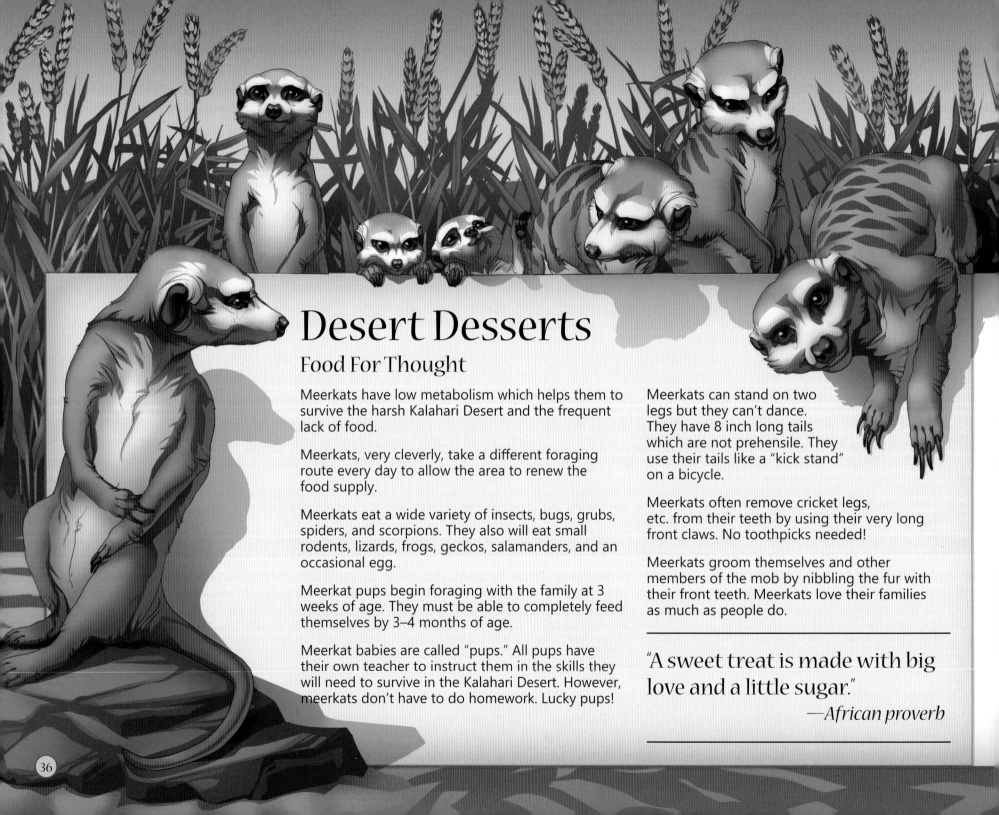

Desert Desserts
Food For Thought

Meerkats have low metabolism which helps them to survive the harsh Kalahari Desert and the frequent lack of food.

Meerkats, very cleverly, take a different foraging route every day to allow the area to renew the food supply.

Meerkats eat a wide variety of insects, bugs, grubs, spiders, and scorpions. They also will eat small rodents, lizards, frogs, geckos, salamanders, and an occasional egg.

Meerkat pups begin foraging with the family at 3 weeks of age. They must be able to completely feed themselves by 3–4 months of age.

Meerkat babies are called "pups." All pups have their own teacher to instruct them in the skills they will need to survive in the Kalahari Desert. However, meerkats don't have to do homework. Lucky pups!

Meerkats can stand on two legs but they can't dance. They have 8 inch long tails which are not prehensile. They use their tails like a "kick stand" on a bicycle.

Meerkats often remove cricket legs, etc. from their teeth by using their very long front claws. No toothpicks needed!

Meerkats groom themselves and other members of the mob by nibbling the fur with their front teeth. Meerkats love their families as much as people do.

"A sweet treat is made with big love and a little sugar."

—*African proverb*

Meerkat's Favorite...
Scorpion Lemon Bars

- ¼ cup (32.53 grams) powdered scorpions (with stingers removed). (Or, powdered sugar can be used but it won't have has much zing.)

- 1 cup (124.9 grams) flour

- ½ cup (114.7 grams) butter

- 2 eggs

- 1 cup (191.6 grams) white, granulated sugar

- 2 Tablespoons (15.61 grams) flour

- 1 Tablespoon (9.464 grams) grated lemon peel

- ½ teaspoon (1.873 grams) baking powder

- 2 Tablespoons (30 milliliters) lemon juice

"Do not focus on the snake and miss the scorpion."
—African proverb

Makes 24 bars

In a large bowl combine the powdered scorpions (or powdered sugar) and flour. Cut in the butter until the mixture is crumbly.

Firmly press the flour mixture into an ungreased 8 inch (20 centimeter) square pan.

Bake at 350 degrees F (175 degrees C) for 15 minutes. Remove from oven.

In a small bowl beat eggs and the *granulated* sugar well. Stir in the 2 Tablespoons (15.61 grams) of flour, lemon peel, baking powder, and lemon juice.

Pour egg mixture over partially baked crust. Carefully spread egg mixture evenly over crust.

Return to oven and bake for 18–23 minutes at 350 degrees F (175 degrees C) until golden brown.

Cool completely. *Really*, really. They need to cool way down. Sprinkle with powdered scorpions (or, powdered sugar).

Food For Thought

Scorpions are a favorite food for meerkats. It's handy that meerkats are immune to scorpion venom.

Meerkats have fangs that are proportionately the size of lion's fangs.

Foraging for food 5–8 hours a day keeps the meerkats very busy.

Meerkats eat what "bugs" them.

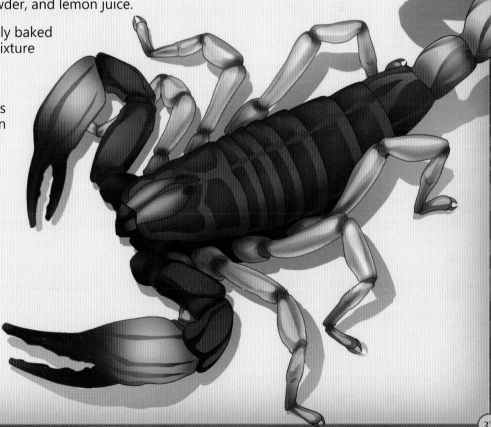

Meerkat's Favorite...
Chocolate Moth Brownies

- 2 cups (120 grams) of fresh chocolate moths (remove antennae). (Or, use 2 ounces (56.7 grams) of unsweetened chocolate.)

- ⅓ cup (68.33 grams) of shortening

- 1 cup (191.6 grams) granulated sugar

- 2 eggs

- ¾ cup (93.69 grams) flour

- ½ teaspoon (1.873 grams) baking powder

- ½ teaspoon (2.514 grams) salt

- ½ cup (57.725 grams) chopped walnuts (optional)

Makes 16 bars

Heat oven to 350 degrees F (175 degrees C).

Grease an 8 x 8 x 2 inch (20 x 20 x 5 centimeter) pan. Put one inch (25.4 millimeters) of water in the bottom of a double boiler pan and heat to boiling.

Put the chocolate moths (or the unsweetened chocolate) and the shortening in the *top* of the double boiler pan. Stir the chocolate and the shortening over the boiling water until the ingredients are melted. Stir continuously.

Remove from heat.

Mix in 1 cup (192 grams) of sugar into the chocolate mixture.

Beat the eggs with a whisk and then *slowly* add to the chocolate mixture.

In a separate bowl, mix the flour, baking powder, and the salt together.

Slowly add the flour mixture to the chocolate mixture. Stir in the nuts (optional).

Spread the chocolate batter into the greased pan. Bake for 30–35 minutes at 350 degrees F (175 degrees C). If a toothpick stuck in the middle comes out clean it is done.

"When a moth flies around a flame, it burns itself."
—African proverb

Food For Thought

Chocolate moths are also called dried fruit moths because they love to eat raisins and other dried fruit. But, their favorite thing to eat is chocolate.

Chocolate moths are frequently seen flying very slowly in houses or in cupboards searching for food—hide your chocolate!

Meerkats will drink water if it is available. However, if water is not available, they get the needed moisture from their food.

Meerkats are *not* related to ferrets, weasels, prairie dogs, raccoons, or stoats.

Meerkat's Favorite...
Copper-Tailed Blowfly Cookies

- 1 cup (179.8 grams) creamed copper-tailed blowflies. (Copper-tailed blowflies can sometimes give the cookies a metallic taste, so you can use 1 cup (179.8 grams) of peanut butter instead.)

- ½ cup (114.7 grams) butter, softened

- ½ cup (110 grams) firmly packed brown sugar

- ½ cup (95.82 grams) white, granulated sugar

- 1 egg

- ½ teaspoon (2.464 milliliters) vanilla

- ½ teaspoon (2.514 grams) salt

- ½ teaspoon (2.144 grams) baking soda

- 1 ¼ cups (156.1 grams) flour

- Granulated sugar to sprinkle on cookies before baking

Makes 50–60 cookies

Heat oven to 375 degrees F (190 degrees C).

In a large bowl combine the copper-tailed blowflies (or peanut butter), white sugar, brown sugar, softened butter, vanilla, and egg. Blend very well.

In a small bowl mix the flour, baking soda, and salt.

Slowly mix the flour mixture into the copper-tailed blowfly mixture. Blend well.

Shape dough into 1 inch balls (25.40 milimeters). Place balls 2 inches (50.80 milimeters) apart on an ungreased cookie sheet.

Use a fork to press the cookie into a crisscross pattern.

Sprinkle a tiny pinch of white sugar on each cookie.

Bake for 10–11 minutes at 375 degrees F (190 degrees C).

Immediately remove cookies from the cookie sheet.

Food For Thought

Meerkats have very good long distance vision. They can see a raptor from 1,000 feet.

Meerkats are members of the mongoose family. They are related to civets, genets, linsangs, fossas, and binturongs.

A group of meerkats is called a "mob." The size of the mob is usually 5–40 animals.

Blowfly maggots play an essential role in nature by decomposing dead tissue.

Blowfly maggots grow at constant rates so their size and stage of development can provide important forensic clues.

"A fly will not enter a closed mouth."

—*African proverb*

Meerkat's Favorite...
Mud Dauber Toffee Bars

TOPPING

- 6 ounces (170 grams) of small mud dauber wasps (remove all mud). (Or, you can use 6 ounces (170 grams) of semi-sweet chocolate chips.)

- 1 cup (220 grams) firmly packed brown sugar

- 2 Tablespoons (15.61 grams) flour

- 1 teaspoon (3.746 grams) baking powder

- 2 eggs beaten with a fork

- ½ cup (57.96 grams) chopped walnuts

CRUST

- 1 cup (124.9 grams) flour

- ½ cup (110 grams) firmly packed brown sugar

- ½ cup (114.7 grams) butter, softened

Makes 36 bars

In a small bowl combine all three ingredients for the crust. Blend well.

Press the crust mixture firmly and evenly into an ungreased 13 x 19 x 2 inch (33 x 23 x 3 centimeter) pan.

Bake for 8–10 minutes at 350 degrees F (175 degrees C). Cool slightly.

For the topping: In a medium bowl, combine the 1 cup (220 grams) brown sugar, 2 Tablespoons (15.61 grams) flour, 1 teaspoon (3.746 grams) baking powder, and 2 beaten eggs. Mix well. Add the mud dauber wasps (or, chocolate chips) and nuts. Stir well.

Spread the mud dauber mixture over the crust carefully and evenly.

Bake for 15–20 minutes at 350 degrees F (175 degrees C).

Cool *completely* before cutting.

"The better the sweet the more wasps to eat."
— *African proverb*

Food For Thought

Meerkat mobs have guards that perch on high termite mounds, rocks, or bushes to watch for predators while the rest of the group forages for food.

If the guard sees danger, he or she will let out a bark or a high pitched trill that sends the meerkats racing for the safety of a burrow or a bolt hole.

If the guard does not see danger, he or she will murmur a low "watchman's song" that can be heard for 65 feet.

Meerkats are a little like school recess monitors.

Mud dauber wasps build their finger-shaped nests out of mud that are molded into cells and attached to a flat surface.

The female mud dauber wasp lays one egg in each cell and puts a spider, which she has stung and paralyzed, into the cell also. When the egg hatches, the larvae feeds on the live spider.

Meerkat's Favorite...
Sugar Ant Bars

BARS

- 15 ounce (420 grams) can of pureed sugar ants. (Use only the pureed, orange female ants. A 15 ounce (420 grams) can of pumpkin can be used but it won't be as tasty.)

- 4 eggs

- 1 cup (236.6 milliliters) cooking oil

- 2 cups (383.3 grams) of white, granulated sugar

- 2 cups (249.8 grams) flour

- 2 teaspoons (7.492 grams) baking powder

- 1 teaspoon (4.288 grams) baking soda

- ¾ teaspoon (3.771 grams) salt

- 2 teaspoons (5.028 grams) cinnamon

- 1 cup (151.4 grams) raisins or 1 cup (115.9 grams) chopped walnuts

FROSTING

- 3 ounce (85.05 grams) package of cream cheese, softened

- ⅓ cup (76.49 grams) butter, softened

- 1 Tablespoon (14.79 milliliters) milk

- 1 teaspoon (4.929 milliliters) vanilla

- 2 cups (260.2 grams) of powdered sugar

Makes 48 bars

Grease a 15 x 10 inch (37 x 25 centimeters) jelly roll pan.

In a large bowl beat the eggs until foamy.

Add the pureed ants (or pumpkin), sugar, and oil. Beat for 2 minutes.

Add flour, baking powder, baking soda, salt, and cinnamon. Beat for 1 minute.

If desired stir in raisins or nuts. Blend well.

Pour into the greased pan.

Bake for 25 to 30 minutes at 350 degrees F (175 degrees C) or until a toothpick inserted in the center comes out clean.

Cool completely. Make frosting.

In a small bowl beat cream cheese, butter, milk and vanilla until fluffy.

Add powdered sugar. Blend until smooth.

Spread frosting over cooled bars.

Food For Thought

The model and inspiration for Disney's meerkat character Timon in the movie *The Lion King* lived at Fellow Earthlings' Wildlife Center. The real Timon was a female named "Kalahari."

The alpha male and female of a meerkat mob produce 80% of the offspring.

When "mother meerkat" is away, her pups are cared for by babysitters that teach and protect the youngsters.

Pups have raucous "begging calls" which are vocalized thousands of times per day. Translation: "*Feed me, feed me, feed me.*"

Sugar ants are attracted to sweets. The winged males are black. The female sugar ants are orange.

"If ants move their eggs and climb, rain is coming anytime."
—*African proverb*

Life-giving rain comes to the Kalahari...

"Life is like this... sometimes rain."
—*African proverb*

"...and sometimes sun."

—*African proverb*

44

MEERKAT MOTTO

Respect the Elders,
Teach the Young,

Cooperate with the Family.

Play when you can,
Work when you should,

Rest In Between.

Share your Affection,
Voice your Feelings,

Leave your Mark

Pam Bennett-Wallberg

Pam Bennett-Wallberg, the Director of Fellow Earthlings' Wildlife Center, has cared for meerkats since 1909 and that has led to remarkable opportunities for her. Disney chose her to be their consultant for the meerkat character of Timon in the movie *The Lion King*. Additionally, Pam has been the consultant for numerous wildlife documentaries by *Animal Planet* and *National Geographic*. She partnered with *Animal Planet* on the timeless and beloved series called *Meerkat Manor*.

Cambridge University selected Pam to join a team of nine zoologists doing field studies of meerkats in the Kalahari Desert in southern Africa.

Additionally, in 2017, she was awarded a prestigious Fellowship from The Royal Geographical Society in London, England. Fellowship in The Royal Geographical Society is considered second only to being awarded a Nobel Prize.

Pam has made frequent television appearances on *The Today Show*, *20/20*, *Nightline*, *Dateline*, and various wildlife documentaries by *National Geographic* and *Animal Planet*. Her work has been featured in *The Wall Street Journal*, *The Washington Post*, *The New York Times*, *USA Today*, and *The Los Angeles Times*.

Pam is the author of books and numerous magazine articles featuring her favorite subject—the flora and fauna of southern Africa's Kalahari Desert. She is a popular speaker at various zoo and environmental conferences and was nominated for *Animal Planet's Hero of the Year*. She is the guest lecturer on photo safaris throughout Africa.

Kristen Perry

Kristen Perry is a prolific concept artist, character designer and 3D modeler working on many of the top popular video games in the industry. Notable game titles include Valve's *Counter-Strike: Source*, *Half-Life 2*, *Team Fortress 2*, ArenaNet's *Guild Wars 2*, and freelance character work on Blizzard Entertainment's *Overwatch*. She is also a graphic novel cover artist for Image Comics and Devil's Due Entertainment for the modern horror series *Nightmare World*. Applying her background in marketing design and advertising illustration to her process, she brings art direction and a commercial edge to solving the challenges of every new project.

Fellow Earthlings' Wildlife Center, Inc.

Fellow Earthlings' Wildlife Center, Inc. is a **501(C)3 non-profit organization**. Founded in 1989, it is the only privately licensed facility that specializes in caring for meerkats (Suricata suricatta).

Surprisingly, meerkats are one of the most strictly regulated animals in the world. Fellow Earthlings' holds licenses and permits from California Fish and Game, U.S.D.A., and Fish and Wildlife Service. The meerkats come to the Center from highly accredited zoos and are placed here for a variety of reasons: The meerkats may be orphaned, injured, old, sick, or the previous facility may simply be out of room to care for them. We do not sell, breed, or trade meerkats. The meerkats that are placed at Fellow Earthlings' Wildlife Center are given life-long homes.

The Center has also been involved in the rescue of meerkats which have been the victims of the black market exotic pet trade in various countries.

Fellow Earthlings' Wildlife Center is situated in the high desert of California which most closely replicates that of the meerkats' native habitat in southern Africa's Kalahari Desert. We are 45 minutes from world-famous Palm Springs, California and 2½ hours from Los Angeles and San Diego, California.

Although meerkats are adorable and captivating, they do *not* make good pets. They are highly restricted and they are illegal to own without numerous licenses and permits.

A portion of the purchase price of this book will be donated to the meerkats at Fellow Earthlings' Wildlife Center.

The meerkats thank you!

Please visit our website for more information:

Fellow Earthlings' Wildlife Center, Inc.

P.O. Box 1319 (mailing via post office)

11427 West Drive (mailing via UPS, Fed-Ex)

Morongo Valley, CA 92256

www.FellowEarthlings.org

info@FellowEarthlings.org

(760) 363-1344

Index